RASPBERRIES!

AN AMERICAN TALE OF COOPERATION

Three yellow birds lived in a hedge.
Two flew away: **Loop-de-loop! Loop-de-loop!**

The third bird had only one wing
and could not fly.
"Tweet-tweet! Tweet-tweet!" she sang sadly.

Pitter-pat! Pitter-pat!
A little dog trotted up to the hedge.
"Why the sad song?" he inquired.

"My brothers are flying
Loop-de-loop! Loop-de-loop!
to the raspberry bush across the street,"
sighed the little bird, "and they have left me
here all alone."

"We can get there on foot," said the little dog.
So the bird and the dog hip-hop, trip-trotted
along the sidewalk.
Pitter-pat! Pitter-pat!
Tweet-tweet! Tweet-tweet!

At the corner, traffic zipped by.

Beep-beep!   **Honk-honk!**
     Zoom-zoom!   **WHOOSH!!**

"TWEET-TWEET!"
cried the little bird, afraid for her life.

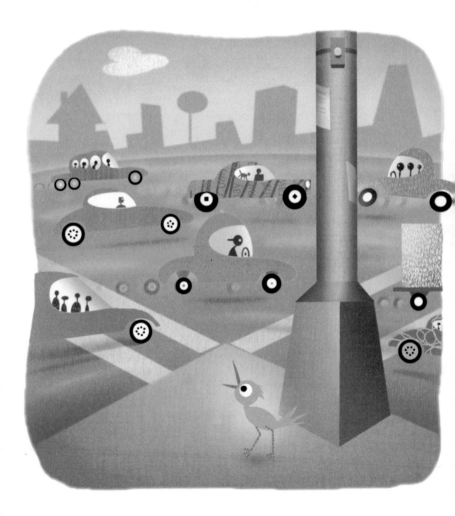

"We have to press the button,"
said the little dog.
"Then the traffic light will turn red, the cars
will stop, and it will be safe to cross the street."

The little bird jumped up and jumped up,
but she couldn't reach the button.

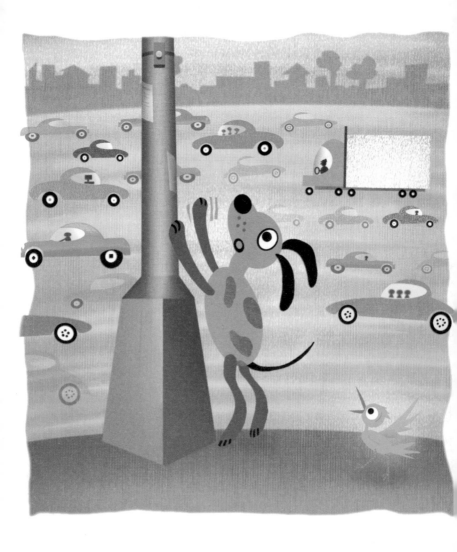

The little dog reared up on his hind legs.
He poked with his paws,
nudged with his nose,
and even swatted with his tail, but he
couldn't reach it, either.

Traffic zipped by.
Beep-beep!   **Honk-honk!**
   Zoom-zoom!   **WHOOSH!!**

"Chit-chatter! Chit-chatter!"

"What are you two up to?"
asked a chatty chipmunk.

"We are trying to cross the street to get some
delicious raspberries," said the bird,
"but we can't reach the walk signal button."

"I'll shimmy on up and press that button!" the chipmunk said. She shimmied, but the pole was too smooth, and she slid and she slid back down.

Traffic zipped by.

Beep-beep! **Honk-honk!**
  Zoom-zoom! **WHOOSH!!**

Along came a frog,
flippity-flop, flippity-flop.
"Whatcha doin'?" asked the frog.

"We want to cross the street,
but we can't reach the walk signal button,"
explained the little bird.

"Lemme try!" said the frog.
He jumped and he jumped,
flapping his floppy feet.
He even tried with his long, long tongue,
but he couldn't reach it, either.

Traffic zipped by.
Beep-beep!   **Honk-honk!**
Zoom-zoom!   **WHOOSH!!**

"I have an idea!" chirped the little bird,
hip-hopping all around.
"Everyone lie down!"
"Lie down?!" said the dog,
the chipmunk and the frog.
"Don't we want to be taller?"
"Exactly!" said the bird.
She stepped onto the frog.
"Hee-hee! That tickles!" giggled the frog.
"Now hop onto the chipmunk,"
instructed the little bird.

So the frog, with the bird on his back,
hopped onto the chipmunk.
"Oooophf! You're heavier than you look!"
groaned the chipmunk.
"Now climb onto the dog," said the little bird.

So the chipmunk, with the frog and
the bird on her back, climbed onto the dog.
"Ouch!" yipped the dog.
"Try not to pull my hair!"
But the chipmunk hung on
to the dog's fur for dear life.
"Now stand up!" said the little bird.

So the dog, with the chipmunk,
the frog, and the bird on his back,
slooowly stood up.
They balanced like acrobats in a circus.

Traffic zipped by.
**Beep-beep!   Honk-honk!
     Zoom-zoom!   WHOOSH!**

The little bird pecked the button,
and the light turned red.
Traffic stopped. It was quiet.
The dog, the chipmunk, the frog,
and the bird looked this way.
They looked that way.
The walk signal said, "Walk!" So they did.

Pitter-pat, pitter-pat.
Swaaay-o,
Wibble-wobble!
Tweet! Tweet!

That was quite a sight! But nobody saw them do it. Just at that moment, the driver coming this way looked down to change the radio station in his car. The driver going that way consulted her map.

When they reached the other side, the dog slooowly kneeled down and the bird, the frog, and the chipmunk hopped off and raced to the raspberry bush:

Tweet-tweet! Tweet-tweet!
Pitter-pat! Pitter-pat!
Chit-chatter! Chit-chatter!
Flippity-flop! Flippity-flop!
Loop-de-loop! Loop-de-loop!

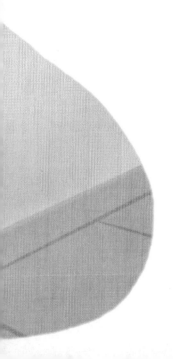

Where they ate
delicious raspberries
all day long.

THE END